the REINDEER Wish

By Lori Evert

Photographs by Per Breiehagen

Random House  New York

$\mathcal{L}$ong, long ago, far to the north and high in the snowy mountains, where you could ski for days and never see another soul, lived a kind little girl named Anja.

Anja had many friends at school, but when school was out she sometimes got lonely. She would have liked to have a brother or a sister; but mostly she wished for a puppy. Every week, she wrote a letter to Santa, put it in the postbox, and hoped for the best.

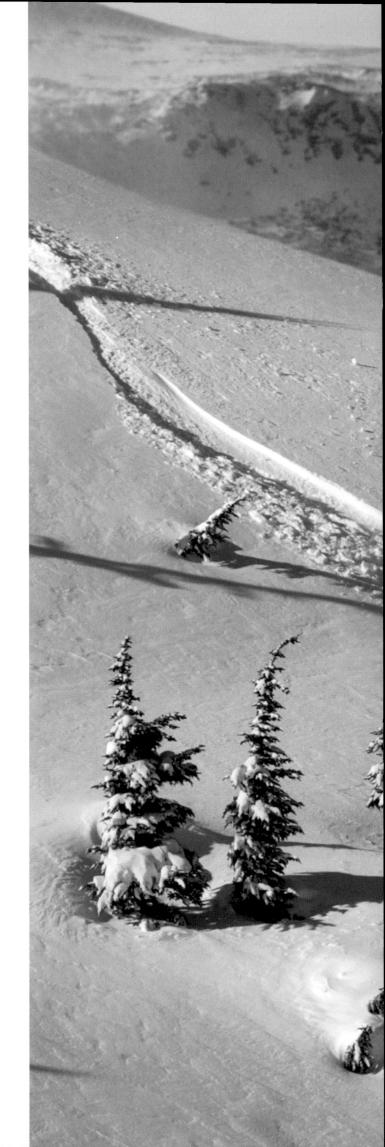

One Christmas Eve, while her parents were busy getting ready for the holiday, Anja took a little trip to the one hill that she was allowed to ski alone. She climbed up that hill and flew back down, over and over again, until the day's light began to fade and she became quite cold and tired.

FOR OUR KIND, BRAVE ANJA
AND ALL HER FRIENDS

Special thanks to Brad Palm, Cheryl Meyer, Øystein, Guri Sissel, Hanna, Petter,
Nora, and Anna. Also to Jan and Eivind and to their lovely reindeer.

Book Designer: Cheryl Meyer
Digital Artists: Per Breiehagen and Brad Palm
Santa Claus: Robert J. Fleskes

Text copyright © 2015 by Lori Evert
Jacket and interior photographs copyright © 2015 by Per Breiehagen

Visit us on the Web! randomhousekids.com
Educators and librarians, for a variety of teaching tools, visit us at RHTeachersLibrarians.com

For additional information about this book, visit www.TheChristmasWish.net

Library of Congress Cataloging-in-Publication Data
The reindeer wish / story by Lori Evert ; photographs by Per Breiehagen. —
First edition.
pages cm.
ISBN 978-0-385-37921-2 (trade) — ISBN 978-0-375-97335-2 (lib. bdg.) —
ISBN 978-0-375-98236-1 (ebook)
[1. Wishes—Fiction. 2. Reindeer—Fiction. 3. Christmas—Fiction.
4. Arctic regions—Fiction.] I. Breiehagen, Per, illustrator. II. Title.
PZ7.E927Rei 2015 [Fic]—dc23 2014032999

MANUFACTURED IN CHINA
10 9 8 7 6 5 4 3 2 1
First Edition

Anja decided to rest until
her mother came to take her home.
She had learned that animals keep
warm by burying themselves in snow,
so she set up her skis, then burrowed
into a little hole under a tree, and
drifted off to sleep.

When Anja woke, she saw a cardinal—
a rare sight so far north. She wondered
if this was the cardinal who had helped
her meet Santa Claus the Christmas
before. Then the cardinal spoke.
It *was* that cardinal!

The bird said, "Anja, I need your help. There is a baby reindeer alone under a tree near your house. Can you get your sled and help me save him?" Anja skied home, grabbed her sled, and followed the cardinal to the baby.

As she followed him, Anja worried about taking the little reindeer; she had been told never to touch a wild baby animal. The cardinal told her that the mother reindeer could not come back. "He will starve if we leave him," the cardinal said. "You must take him home and care for him."

Anja looked at the reindeer. "What a beautiful little baby," she thought. She gently picked him up and he nuzzled into her neck. "I hope I can keep him," she told the cardinal.

The bird assured Anja that her parents would not turn the reindeer away.

The cardinal was right; Anja's parents told her that she would be a very good reindeer mama, and that the baby could sleep in the little hay shed. After a great deal of thought, she named him Odin, after her grandfather. Anja spent every free moment with her young friend; she fed Odin with a baby bottle, sang to him, and played her fiddle for him. He grew stronger each day.

Winter flew by as Anja and Odin played and raced and looked for signs of spring. As the lake thawed, they loved to watch the swans and laughed as the usually graceful birds dove for food, bottoms up and feet flapping.

$\mathscr{A}$s Odin grew, so did
his antlers. He could not
guess how Anja always found
him when they played hide-
and-seek.

They spent the spring
and summer exploring the
countryside, often stopping
for a chat and a snack.

Anja's grandfather had told her that the best place to practice her fiddle was alongside the music of a waterfall. Every morning, Odin followed Anja to the rushing, splashing falls, where she played beautiful tunes for him, the squirrels, and the birds.

Odin was a wonderful fishing partner as well; they roamed far into the mountains, searching for trout and taking a dip if the day got warm.

One day while Anja was fishing, Odin
wandered away, following a delicious trail of
reindeer moss. She searched and called for
him, and she became very worried. Finally,
she ran back to her house and found the
wooden horn her parents used to call her
home. Anja blew the horn with all her might—
it worked! Odin came trotting back as soon
as he heard the sound.

Autumn came quickly. Odin didn't understand that he wasn't invited into the schoolhouse, and he gave the teacher a fright the first day when he decided to join Anja's class. The children laughed and laughed, long after Anja took Odin outside and asked him to wait for her. Her parents laughed too when she told them the story later.

Autumn is a short season in the mountains; it seems that as soon as your bare feet begin to feel a chill, the first snowflakes appear. Anja realized that Odin was as smart as he was strong, so she began to teach him to pull a sleigh. She started with her little sled, having him pull small loads of dolls and toys, and sometimes she pretended that she was Santa Claus himself!

One day, as Christmas drew near, Anja borrowed her
father's horse sleigh. She and Odin were going to bring
home the loveliest Christmas tree Santa had ever seen!

They decorated the tree
together; what fun they had!
Anja could not resist putting
a few ornaments on Odin's
antlers. He stood perfectly still
and she tried not to laugh—he
looked so festive and silly!

The next day was colder—a perfect day to ice-skate. Odin was an attentive audience. He watched as Anja gave one grand performance after another.

After Anja finished skating, as she and Odin happily made their way home, they suddenly heard a rumble from above. They looked up and saw a reindeer herd running along the ridge. Anja turned to tell Odin that it was the most beautiful sight she had ever seen, but she stopped short when she saw a tear in Odin's eye.

Anja wondered then if Odin missed living with other reindeer. Would he be happier if he could run with that herd? They walked slowly now, each lost in their own thoughts.

As Anja hugged Odin good night, she continued to think about the reindeer herd. It would break her heart to lose her best friend, but she wanted him to be happy. She had never felt so confused before.

That night, Anja couldn't sleep until she remembered the bell Santa had given her. He had said, "If you ever need help, ring this bell three times." She had taken Santa's offer very seriously and had never used the bell. When she woke up the next morning, she went outside and rang the bell. On the third ring, the cardinal appeared.

"Santa has a place for Odin with his herd of magic reindeer. If you wish, I can guide you and Odin to his home at the North Pole," the cardinal said.

They agreed to leave at once.

It was a long journey through snowy white forests and over windy mountain passes. Anja rode on Odin's warm back, and the cardinal sang songs and told them cheerful, funny stories about life at the North Pole.

As evening fell, their path was lit by magical, shimmering ice globes.

Early the next morning, they entered a snowy forest and could see a red house surrounded by reindeer. They passed a grove of trees and there was Santa Claus, arms open in greeting. He hugged them all and said, "Welcome! Thank you, Anja, for your wonderful gift. I am proud of how well you have cared for and trained Odin. I know you will miss each other, but I promise that he will be very happy here and that you will see him every year. I have a gift for you in return." Santa Claus presented a bag with three adorable, squirming puppies, and asked Anja to choose one for herself.

nja picked up the puppy who had reached for her hand, and she was just about to thank Santa when the puppy licked her face, making her laugh instead.

The next thing she knew, Anja was in her own bed, laughing, and the puppy was in her arms!

"How did I get home?" she wondered. "Could it all have been a dream? But if it was a dream, how did this puppy get here?"

What do you think?